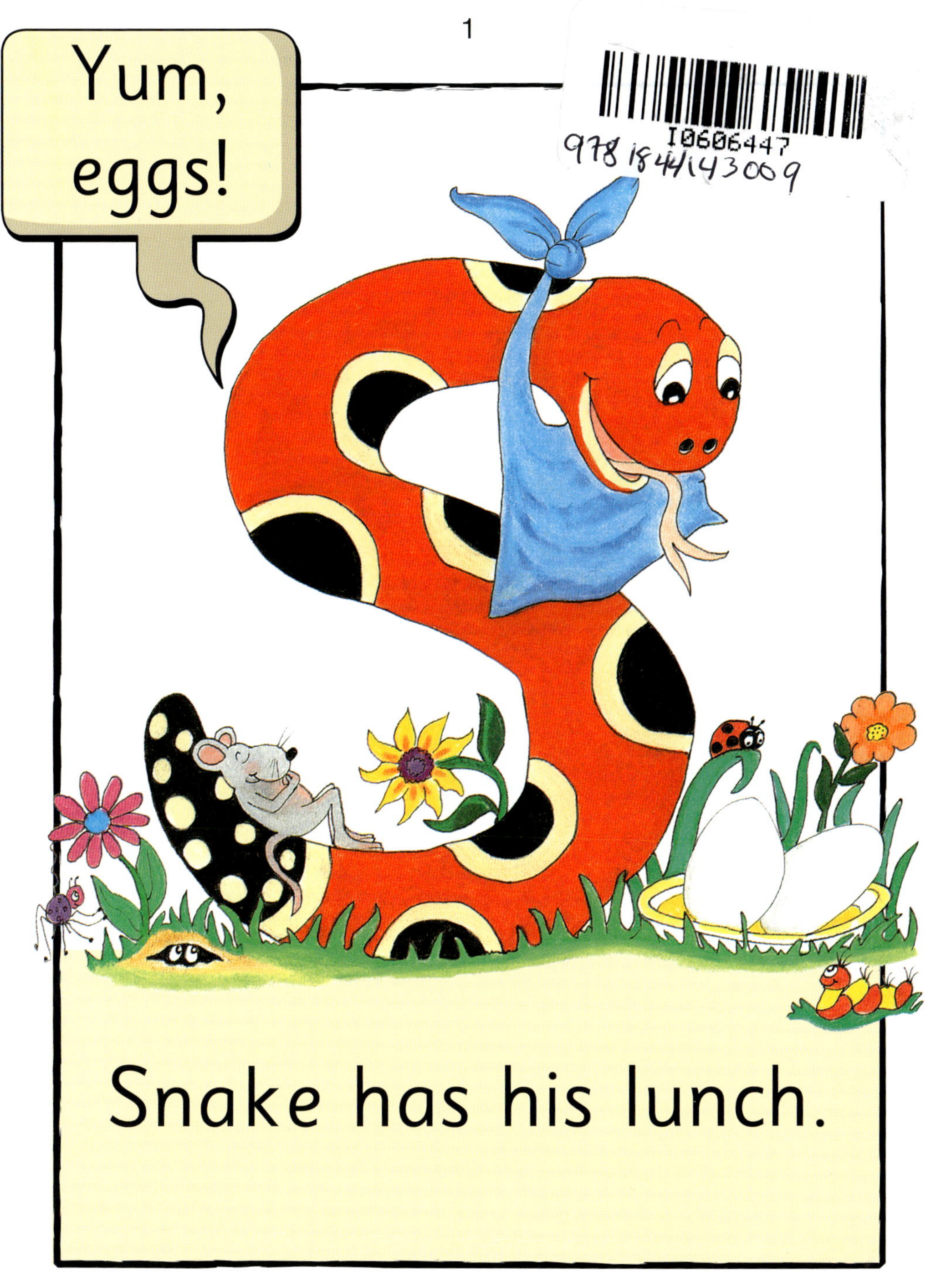

Snake has his lunch.

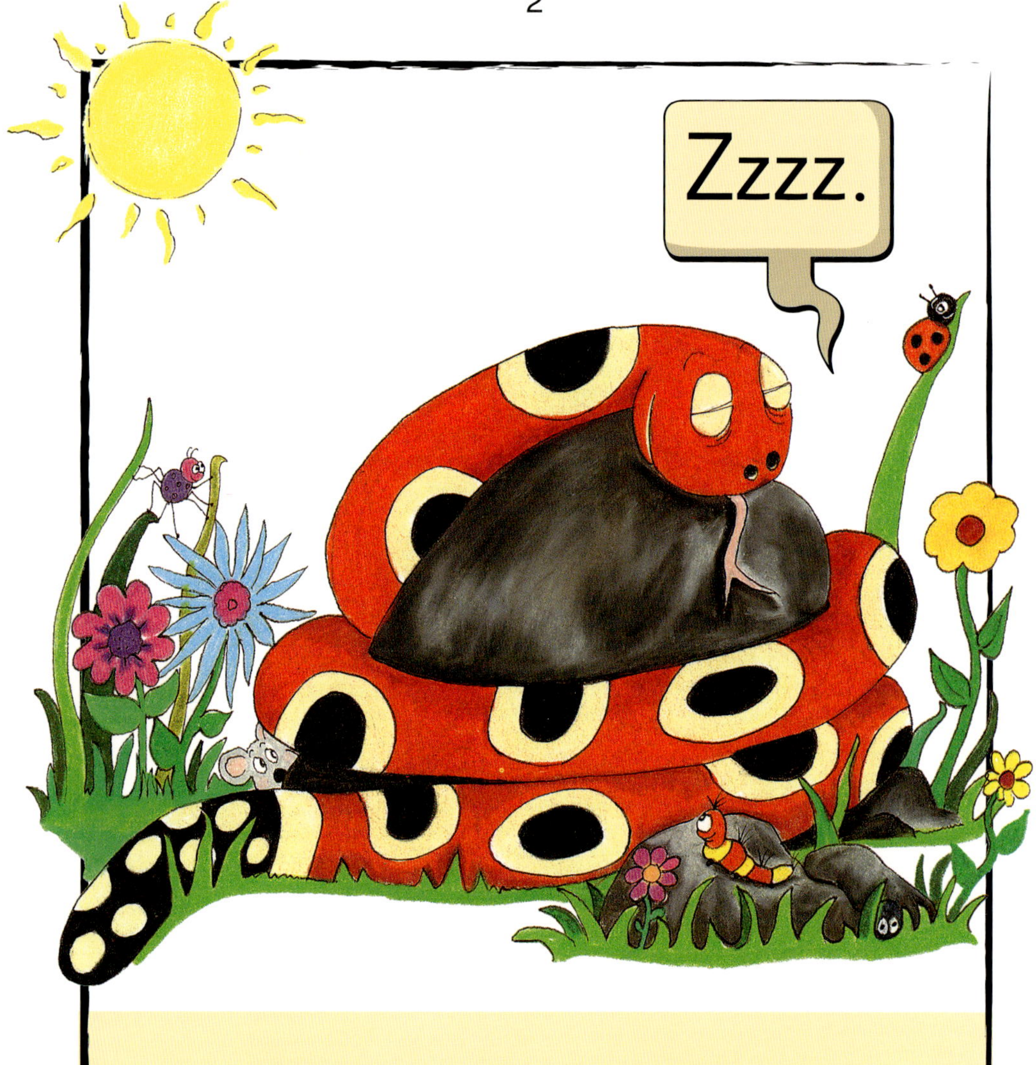

Then he sleeps
in the sun.

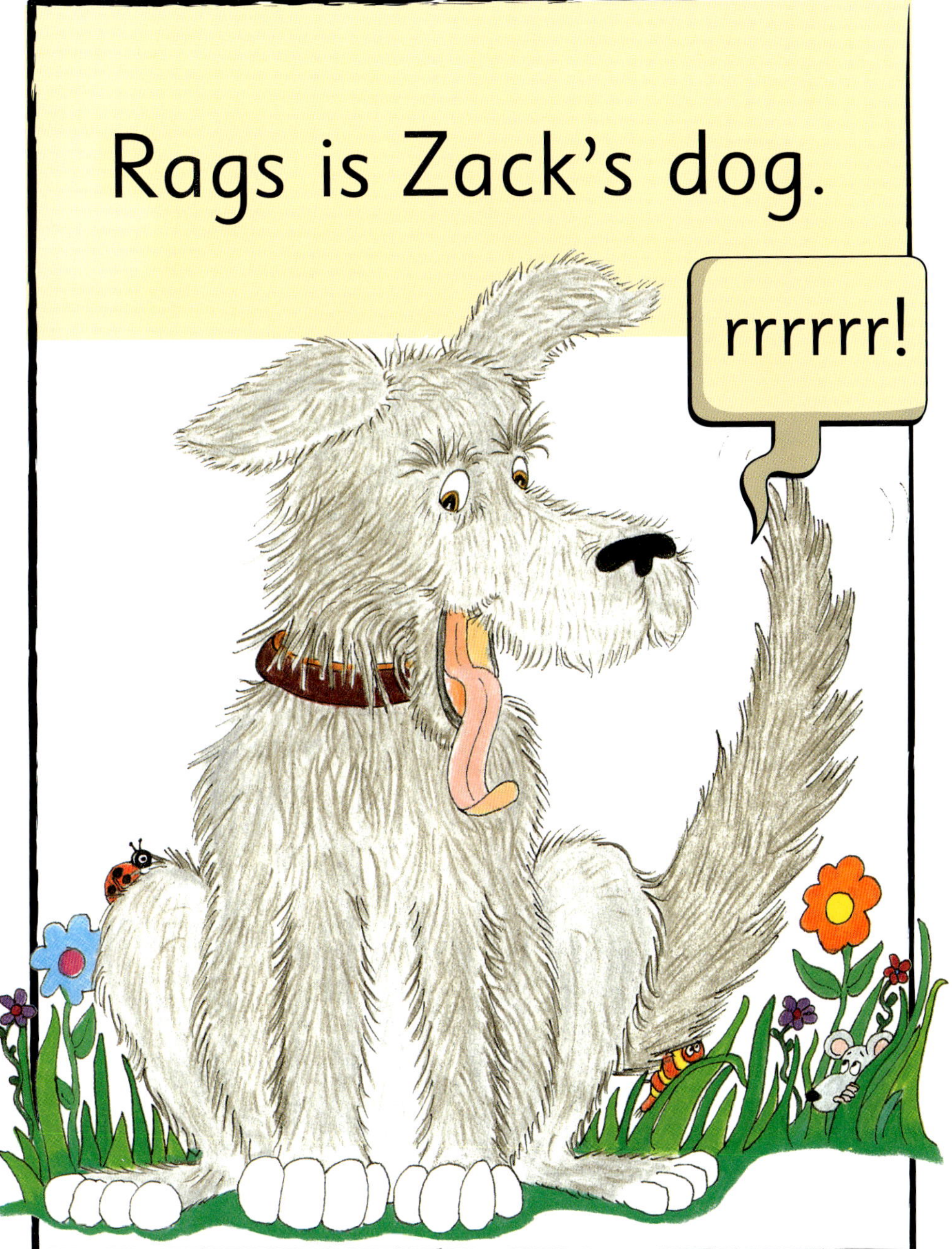
Rags is Zack's dog.
rrrrrr!

Rags is running around and barking.

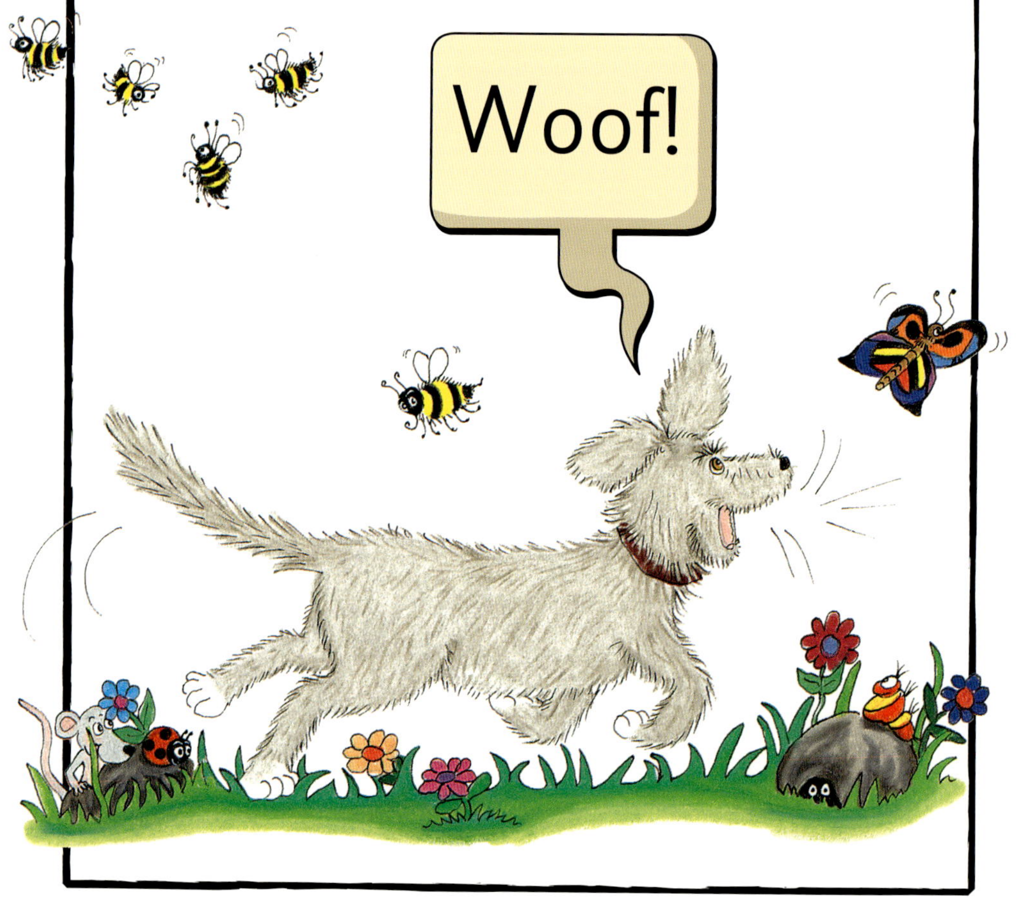

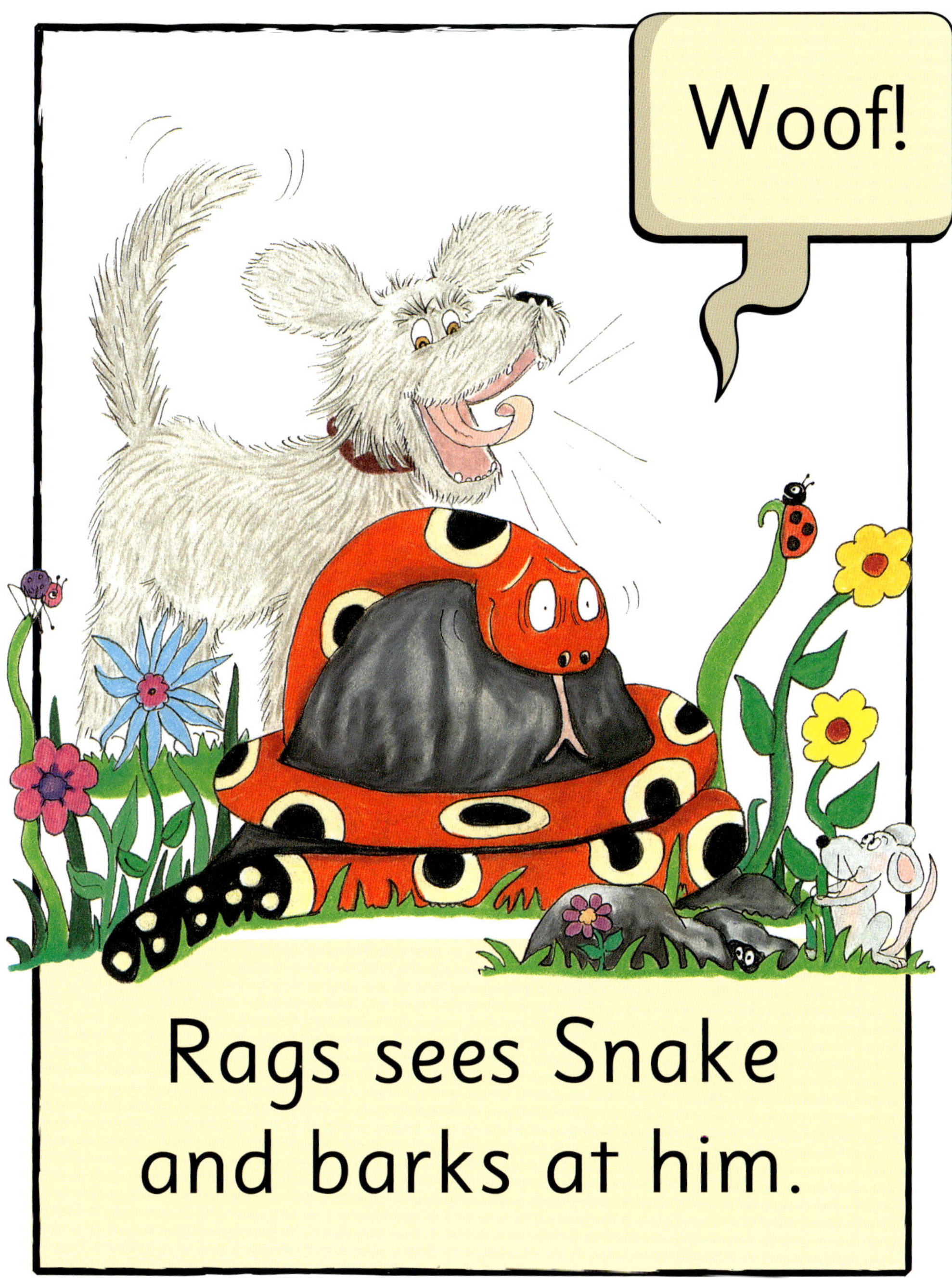

Rags sees Snake
and barks at him.

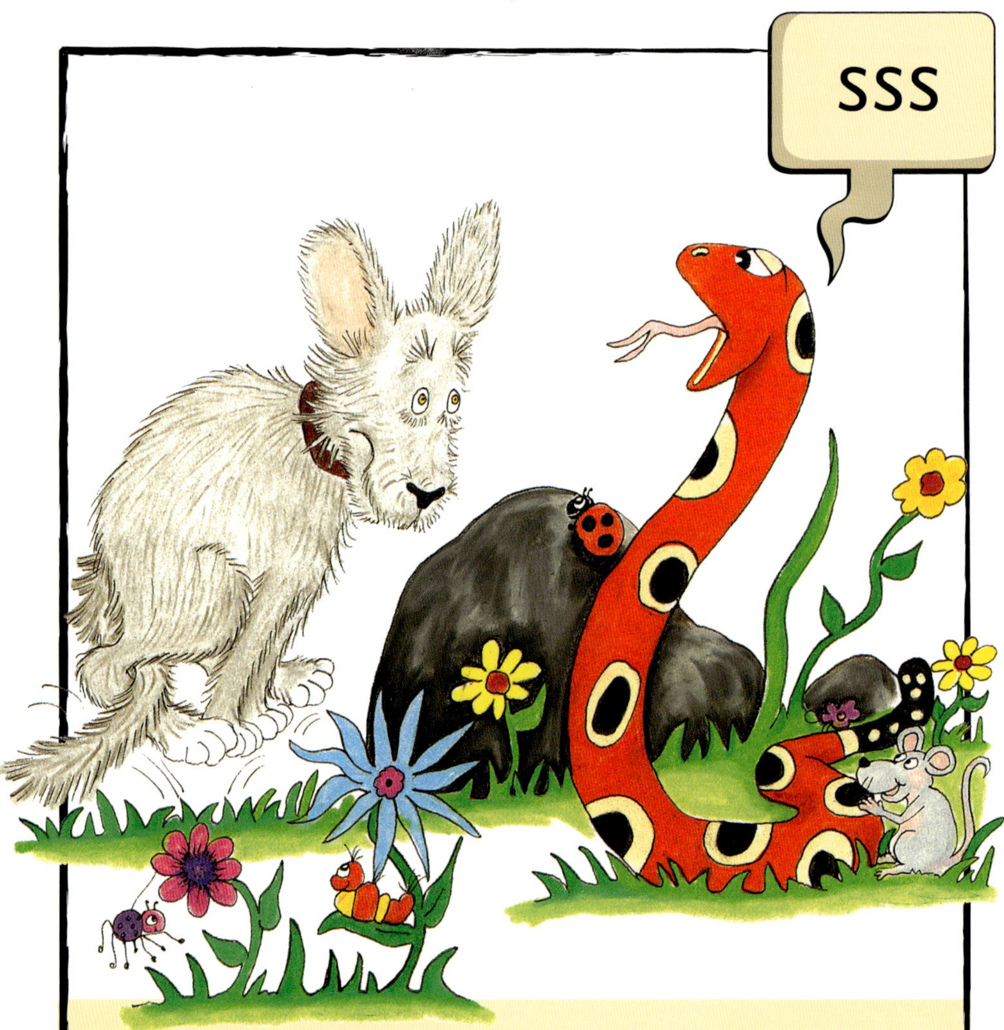

"sss" Snake hisses
and stands up.

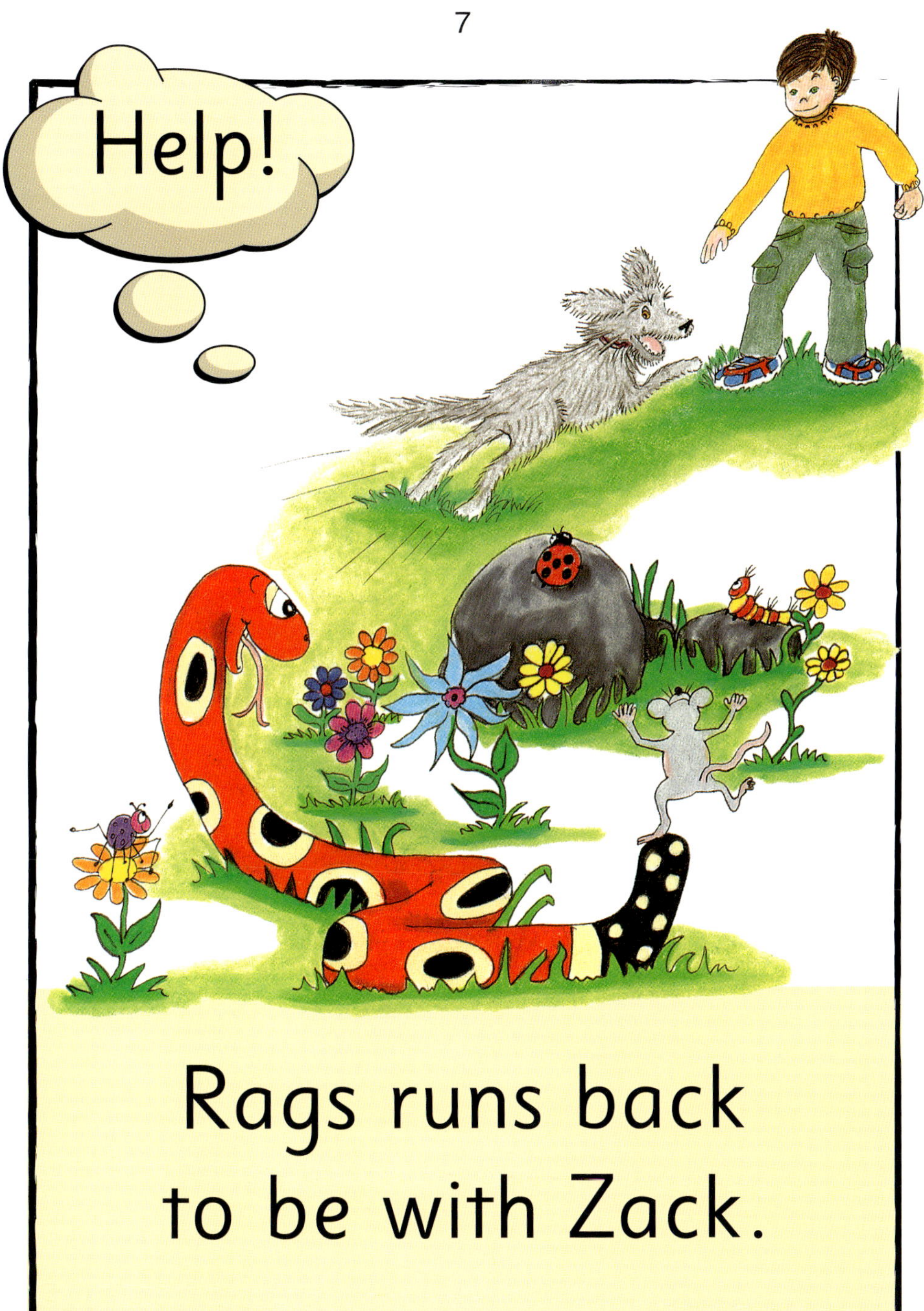

Rags runs back
to be with Zack.

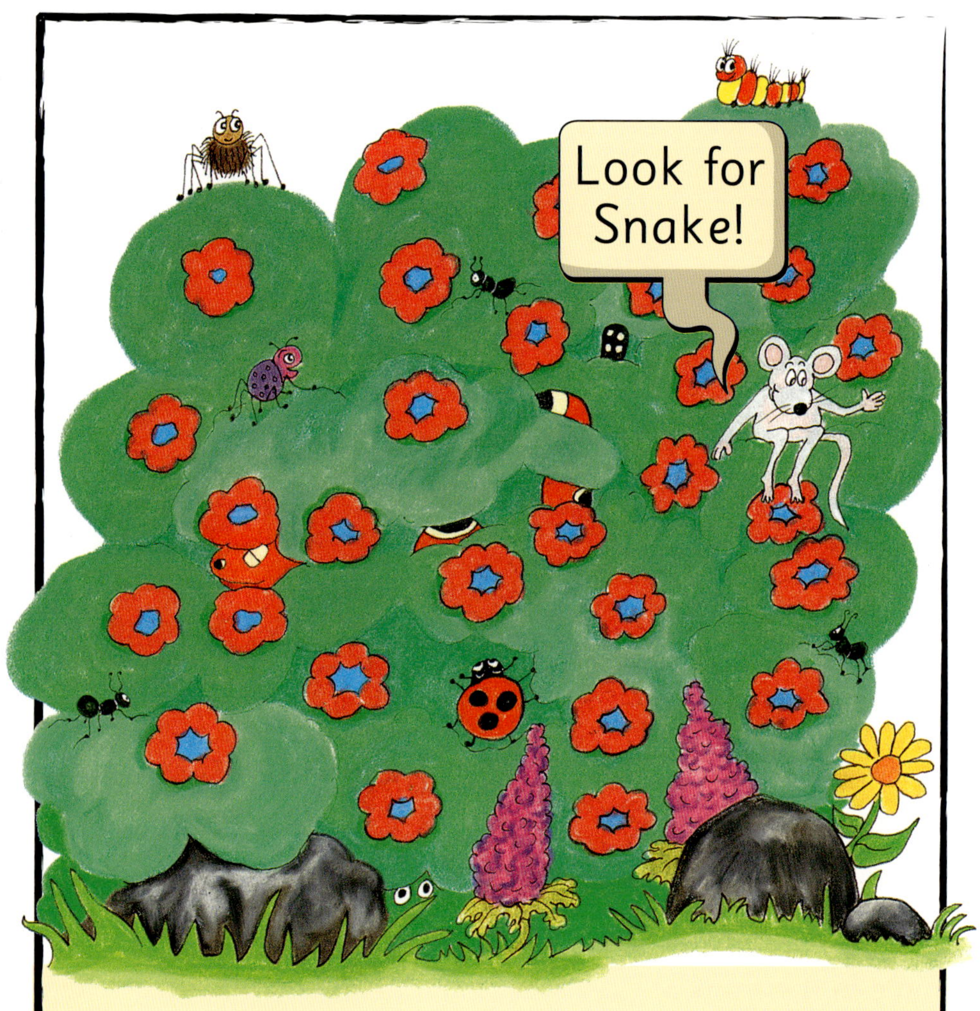

Snake has hidden and is sleeping.